BOOKS BY NATALIE BABBITT

Dick Foote and the Shark

Phoebe's Revolt

The Search for Delicious

Kneeknock Rise

The Something

Goody Hall

The Devil's Storybook

Tuck Everlasting

The Eyes of the Amaryllis

Herbert Rowbarge

The Devil's Other Storybook

Nellie: A Cat on Her Own

Bub, or The Very Best Thing

Elsie Times Eight

Jack Plank Tells Tales

JACK PLANK TELLS TALES

Natalie Babbitt

JACK PLANK TELLS TALES

MICHAEL DI CAPUA BOOKS
SCHOLASTIC

This book is for

TESS AUDLEY BABBITT

My third grandchild

A NOTE
TO THE READER

IT DOESN'T really matter, but in case you're interested, Jack Plank is telling these tales on the island of Jamaica in the Caribbean Sea, around the year 1720. There'd been a lot of pirates in those waters ever since Christopher Columbus came over from Spain, looking for India. India wasn't there, but Columbus did find a lot of islands with a lot of treasure: gold and silver and other nice things. That was very good news to the Spanish king and queen, who sent ships right away to start removing it from the natives it belonged to and bringing it back to Spain. This made things easy for the pirates. They let Spain do the removing so that, later on, they could run down the Spanish ships and grab the lot. After about two hundred years, though, things weren't quite so easy for pirates. There are a lot of reasons why this was so, but never mind. It's just that Jack probably got out of the business at the right time.

———

JACK PLANK TELLS TALES

1

HOW IT ALL BEGAN

JACK PLANK was an out-of-work pirate. He'd had a job, and a good job, too, on a lovely ship called the *Avarice*. But the thing is, Jack wasn't good at plundering. There's only one way to plunder: You have to yell and make faces and rattle your sword, and once you've got people scared, you take things away from them. That's what pirates do. But Jack didn't seem to have a knack for it.

Still, he was used to the life of the open sea, and he was fond of his shipmates, all of whom were just as fond of him, including the quartermaster, Leech, who mostly hated everyone. Even Captain Scudder was fond of him. So he kept his place for a good long time. After a while, though, Captain Scudder told him to stay behind and keep the soup hot while the others were busy plundering, and then, in the evenings, they'd all have supper together and go to sleep happy.

But a hard day came when pirating didn't pay as well as sometimes, and there wasn't always soup enough for everyone. So the captain said to Jack, "Plank, old man, hard days do not allow for sentiment. Like it or not, we're going to have to let you go, for we can't afford to feed any but the plunderers." And of course Jack could see the sense of this, even if it was a disappointment.

Later that same night, with the *Avarice* anchored well offshore from an island port called Saltwash, the crew lowered a longboat, and a bunch of them, including the quartermaster, Leech, rowed Jack in to shore — Jack and his little trunk of keepsakes. "We'll miss you, Jack," said Leech, holding his voice low

so as not to rouse the Saltwash population. "Here's a goodbye present. We all put in a piece." And Leech handed him a small bag of money — gold florins enough, they hoped, to start him in some new direction. Then they patted him on the back and shoved off in the longboat, leaving him behind. Poor Jack watched them go till they'd reached the *Avarice* and boarded her, and he watched as she slipped away, silent as a shadow in the moonlight, away and away till there was nothing left to watch except the lift of the waves and now and then a far-off shooting star.

"Well, that's that, I guess," said Jack. But he didn't give in to feeling sorry for himself. Instead, he wrapped up warm in his cloak, stretched out right there on the beach, and managed to go to sleep. And in the morning, with a bright sun climbing the sky to cheer him, he brushed the sand off his clothes, picked up his little trunk, and with his florins in his pocket made his way into town.

The deepest part of the Saltwash harbor was crowded with docks, ships, and sailors, but Jack didn't pause to watch them working. Instead, he walked about, up and down the streets, looking for a place to live, and settled at last on a boardinghouse that was narrow but tall, and had a window box with bright red flowers and a sign, above the flowers, that said:

ROOMS TO LET

BY THE WEEK, BY THE MONTH

MRS. DELFRESNO, PROPRIETRESS

RING BELL

Jack stepped forward, set down his trunk, and rang the bell. And here came Mrs. DelFresno herself, opening the door to him, a handsome widow, plump and neatly dressed, and she looked him in the eye and said severely, "Yes?"

Jack bowed to the widow, hat in hand, and introduced himself, explaining that he wished to take a room.

"Well, sir," said Mrs. DelFresno, "that's as may be, but it's plain to see you're a pirate, so I'm not entirely sure you'll do."

"I was a pirate once," said Jack, "that's true. But I've put the life aside if not the uniform. King George, across the sea in England, is pardoning all of us who give it up. But now I must try a new career, with a nice place to live while I'm trying."

"Ah!" said Mrs. DelFresno. "That's different, then. Still, I hardly know . . ."

Then here came her daughter, Nina, sharp and smart and eleven years old, and she studied Jack from the doorway. "I like him, Mama," she said at last to her mother. "Let's take him in."

"Well, perhaps," said Mrs. DelFresno, frowning at Jack. "But tell me, Mr. Plank, how will you get along with my other boarders? Old Miss Withers and her uncle? They've been here now for many months, and I must consider their welfare."

"Consider away," said Jack, "and I'll consider with you. That's only fair. But I like the company of others, ma'am, and always did. There won't be any problems, that I promise."

At this, Mrs. DelFresno made up her mind. "Very well, Mr. Plank," she said. "We'll try you out, and if, in a week or so, you've found steady work and proved yourself fit, you may stay as long as you wish. One gold florin a day, please, and supper is at seven."

And Nina said, "I'll help you find the perfect job, Mr. Plank. I can show you around and introduce you, for everyone knows Mama here in Saltwash, and just as many know me."

"My dear," said Jack, "you are very, very kind."

So they all shook hands, the widow and Nina and Jack, and Jack was introduced to old Miss Withers and her uncle and they all shook hands again. Then Jack moved into a pleasant room at the top of the house, where there was one big window looking out to the open sea, and that's how his new life began.

2

NOT
A FARMER

THE NEXT day, at suppertime, Mrs. DelFresno said to Jack, "How did things go with Nina today, Mr. Plank? Did you find suitable work?"

"No, I'm sorry to say I didn't," he told her. "Miss Nina thought I might enjoy the sugarcane fields, and so indeed I might. But there was a problem with the bridge."

"What bridge?" asked the uncle of old Miss Withers, looking up from his supper.

"The bridge that goes over the river to the cane fields," said Nina. "Mr. Plank didn't want to cross it."

"Very sensible," said old Miss Withers, stabbing the air with her fork. "Bridges are always on the edge of falling down."

"Perhaps you're right, ma'am," said Jack, "but you see, I don't use bridges, good or bad."

"What—never?" said Mrs. DelFresno.

"Well, not if I don't have to," said Jack. "The thing is, when I was new to pirating, we had a mate on board the *Avarice* called Lugger who knew a thing or two about bridges. I learned a lot from him."

"What is there to learn about bridges?" said the uncle of old Miss Withers. "Except they keep your feet dry?"

"Tell them what you told me, Mr. Plank," said Nina.

"But, my dear," Jack protested, "I can't think why anyone should care."

"I don't know about caring," said old Miss Withers, "but I insist on an explanation!"

So Jack said, "Very well."

LUGGER WAS some sort of cousin to me—the nephew of a cousin of my mother's, anyway. In fact, he more or less led me into the business. We had just gone up the coast to Newfoundland—there was a lot of good plundering there—and we'd stripped and scuttled a trader and were resting after, when Lugger said he wanted dry land under his feet for a bit. So he rowed himself ashore and climbed a steep hill to the top, and was walking along, keeping an eye out for blueberries, when he came to a pile of rocks heaped across the path. And there, standing on the pile, was a poor skinny creature in a pair of worn-out trousers and no boots at all. Maybe he was young, maybe old—it was hard to tell, said Lugger. But one thing was certain: He was ugly. Just about the ugliest face you'd never want to see. And he held out his skinny arms, and he said, "No passing till you pay the toll. One gold piece, and I want it now. Right *now*."

"Oh!" said Lugger. "I see the way of it. You're a troll."

"I am," said the troll.

"I didn't expect to see trolls up here," said Lugger.

"We're everywhere," said the troll with a touch of pride.

"Well," said Lugger, "I'd pay, of course, except I don't have any gold."

"That's bunk," said the troll. "I saw what you were doing down there." And he pointed to the sea below where the *Avarice* swayed in the tide.

"Nevertheless," said Lugger, "I don't have any gold. Every pocket empty."

The troll looked cross on hearing this. "You'll have to get thrown away, then," he said. "That's the rule." And he grabbed Lugger by the hair and began to try turning him upside down.

But Lugger wasn't so easy as all that. He grabbed a handful of hair himself—the troll's hair. "Don't be silly," he managed to say as they struggled there on the path. "I'm just as big as you are, and if one of us gets thrown away, so does the other."

At this, the troll let go of Lugger's hair, and Lugger let go, too. And then the troll sat himself on one of

the rocks in the pile and stared off down the hillside. "I don't know what's to become of me," he moaned. "I've been up here such a long time, trying my best, and all the while they're waiting for gold, but I never have any to give them."

"Who's waiting?" asked Lugger.

"Why, the others!" said the troll. "You know. The big ones. They're a whole lot bigger than me. Uglier, too. The bigger and uglier the better, is how it works for trolls."

"You'll get bigger and uglier soon," said Lugger kindly, "when you're just a little older."

"Do you really think so?" asked the troll.

"Certainly," said Lugger. "But this is a hard way to get your gold, no matter how big and ugly you are. All people need to do to get away is circle around these rocks and just keep right on going."

"That's the pattern," said the troll. "That's what they all do. Not that there's many of them comes here, you know. Hardly anyone comes. Except at last *you're* here, but you don't have any gold, and you don't care, either, and all I want to do is go home to my mama." And two big tears ran down his cheeks.

"Now, now," said Lugger, "don't be sad. There just might be an answer to your problem." He climbed up onto the pile of rocks and peered along the path. "Isn't that a bit of a stream I see ahead?" he asked. "Where that little bridge is built?"

"That's a river," said the troll, snuffling. "Pretty deep, too. Runs right down into the sea."

"No one can walk around a river," said Lugger.

"I don't suppose they can," said the troll. "But so what? It's of no use to *me* one way or the other."

"It might be, though," said Lugger. "I've heard about trolls. Sometimes they set up business at rivers. You could do that. Just move to the bridge over there, and when people come along, charge them a gold piece for crossing. Everyone would pay if there wasn't any choice. Pay, or get tossed in the river."

"Why, I *could* toss them in, couldn't I?" said the troll, brightening at the thought.

"You could," said Lugger. "And they'd go head over heels and sopping wet, bouncing right down to the sea."

"Bouncing right down to the sea!" crooned the troll. "What a fine sight that would be!"

"Let's go and look, and see if it suits the purpose," said Lugger.

So they did, and the troll was right away delighted. He went to the near end of the bridge and he roared at Lugger, "You there! Pay the toll if you want to cross. One gold piece, and I want it *now*!"

"That's fine!" said Lugger. "That would get you *my* gold. If I had any."

"You haven't got gold?" the troll demanded.

"No gold," said Lugger. "I told you that already." And then, before he had time to back off, the troll grabbed him and tossed him into the river. And there he went, head over heels and sopping wet, bouncing right down to the sea. We fished him out, but he never really got over it.

———

"SO THAT'S why I don't use bridges," said Jack. "I don't much want to meet a troll."

"But, Mr. Plank," said Mrs. DelFresno, "surely you don't think *we* have trolls!"

"You might," said Jack. And then he said, "I guess you never met one."

"No," she replied, "I never did."

"Neither did I," said Jack. "And going by what Lugger said, I don't believe I want to."

"So you think there's a troll under our bridge," said old Miss Withers. "Will wonders never cease."

"I hope they never cease," said her uncle. "I like a good wonder now and then."

"Never mind, Mr. Plank," said Nina. "We'll just try something else."

"Thank you, my dear," said Jack, and they went back to eating their supper.

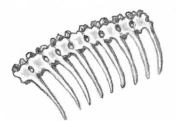

3
NOT
A BAKER

AT SUPPER on the second night, old Miss Withers said to Jack, "The baker has a sign in his window. He's looking for someone to help him."

"Yes, ma'am," said Jack. "Miss Nina and I saw that sign today when we were walking about."

"Well? So?" said old Miss Withers. "Did you ask to be taken on?"

"No, ma'am," said Jack. "As a matter of fact, I didn't."

"Probably you don't know cooking, Plank," said

the uncle of old Miss Withers. "I don't myself, if it comes to that."

"I know a little cooking," said Jack. "I was in charge of soup on the ship—the *Avarice*—and am thereby no stranger to stoves. But all the same, I don't think I'd want to be a baker. Why, just walking up to the shop, and smelling the smell of hot lard and molasses, I was strongly reminded of Spooner. I'm afraid it would always remind me of Spooner, and I don't want to face that every day. Too many questions. Poor Spooner! I never knew whether to laugh at him, or cry."

"Spooner?" said Mrs. DelFresno. "Who was he?"

"Ah, well," said Jack, "who was he, indeed? We never knew exactly."

———

WE CAME across the fellow floating about in a washtub one day, east of the Half Moon Reefs. A hard rain had just swept through, and the sea was still all commotion, but there he sat, without so much as a pole to push with. We hallooed, and

he hallooed back and asked if we had an oven on board. We called to him yes, of course we had an oven, whatever he wanted *that* for, and we reached down a boat hook so as to haul him up. At first he wouldn't grab it. He said that if he came on board, the washtub would have to come, too, since he hoped to be using it later. Leech, the quartermaster, who was out on deck with us — Leech growled that the fellow was clearly a doughhead, but to bring him up anyway. So we hooked on and pulled, and up he came, him and his washtub. We stowed him in the galley to dry, for he was head-to-toe soaked and dripping, and a few of us stayed to hear what he had to say.

Now, you have to understand that, in a way, Leech was right about Spooner: The fellow was a dough-head. And yet, in a way, he wasn't, too. It was easy to see he'd never been a pirate, nothing like, for he didn't look strong or daring. He couldn't have plundered his way across a school yard. And yet, he wasn't afraid of us, though at first it seemed as if Leech would have liked him to be. He told us his name, and then he told us what he wanted: He wanted to bake a cake to please a mermaid.

"Didn't I tell you?" said Leech. "The man's a doughhead."

Spooner paid no attention to this. Instead, he went on with his story. He'd been out fishing the day before, he told us, and he'd seen the mermaid in the Half Moon Reefs. There she sat on a tall rock, combing her hair. "If you gathered up everything charming in all the world," he said, "and rolled it into one, that's what she was. I lost my heart on the spot, and so would you have done, if you'd been there, too, and seen her." Afterwards, he tried to think how to win her, and it came to him that a nice molasses cake might do the trick. So he rounded up the makings, and he baked one and took it to the reefs next morning, in order to set it out on top of the rock where he'd found the mermaid sitting.

"That's when I saw the problem," said Spooner. "I couldn't get close to that rock. The sea thereabouts is too rough for my dory. I feared it'd smash to bits."

"It's too rough for more than dories," said Leech. "Ships are wrecked on those reefs as regular as clockwork."

"Very true," said Spooner.

"Never with me at the helm, though," said Leech, to try him out.

"Well, certainly not," said Spooner. "That goes without saying." At which Leech sat back and didn't look quite so scornful. "So there I was," Spooner went on, "wondering what to do, and that was when I thought of the washtub. I knew I could get up close in a washtub."

He hurried home and fetched one, then made his way back to the dock, where he took up the cake from the dory, climbed with it into the washtub, and pushed off, paddling with a single oar. "And then," he said with a sigh, "it began to rain, very hard—you must have seen it, too—and there was the cake on my knees, open to the elements. I balanced the oar upright in the washtub and started to take off my coat, to cover the cake and keep it dry. But the oar began to lean, and I leaned, too, to save it, and over went the washtub, dumping cake, oar, and me, all three, into the sea."

We whistled at this, for we knew, if anyone does, what it means to go over the side. "Yes," said Spooner, "it was not a happy moment. The oar floated off beyond reach, and the cake turned to mush and sank, and I had all I could do to right the washtub and climb in. But love keeps one hopeful, and rightly so, for all's turned well again. You rescued me, I still have the washtub, and I have in my head the list of needs for another molasses cake. So if your cook will give me the makings, and will let me use his oven, I'll do the work right here. And as soon as it's baked and cooled, I'll set my course back to the reefs with the same high expectations."

We stared at Spooner, all of us, and none of us knew what to say except for Leech, who repeated his opinion that Spooner was a doughhead. But this time he growled it under his breath.

At last the cook—a one-legged man named Stovehouse—at last the cook said, "What's needed for the job, then?"

Spooner ticked off the makings on his fingers. "There's lard," he said, "and molasses, and a bit of brown sugar. And I'd have to have an egg. Would there be an egg on board?"

"There's chickens on board," said Stovehouse, "so of course there's eggs."

"Good," said Spooner. "Then besides all that, I'd only want flour and a little milk. Oh—and a dash of cinnamon."

"Well!" said Stovehouse, opening his eyes very wide. "There's call for a dash of cinnamon, is there? Well, nothing to that! If you'll wait while I step half-way around the world to Java, I'll gladly bring you back some."

Then Leech spoke up. "Come now, Stovehouse, give the man his cinnamon. I know you've got some left from that merchant ship we plundered last July."

It was surprising, hearing this from Leech, for it wasn't like him to be helpful to anyone. But Stovehouse had to follow orders. Leech was the quartermaster, after all. So Spooner got all of his makings, and baked his cake, and the smell of it from the oven floated all over the ship. Even the captain got a happy whiff. And then Spooner wrapped up the cake in his coat, and we lowered him down to the sea with it, all nice and dry in his washtub. I tossed him a long stick of wood for paddling, and away he went, westward, headed for the Half Moon Reefs.

This should have been the end of it. We all believed it was, though we talked about Spooner sometimes and wondered how things had gone for him. "They've stowed him in a madhouse," Leech would say, but we didn't want to hear a thing like that. Instead, we argued the subject of the mermaid. Had there really been a mermaid, out on the rock that day, or had Spooner only made her up? And while we wondered and argued, we held our course south and east, to places good for plundering.

Then, after about a year, we found ourselves once more near the Half Moon Reefs. And one bright morning, when we'd finished with scrubbing the deck, a few of us were lounging at the rail when we saw a washtub bobbing in the water, some little way in the distance but coming steadily nearer.

"Maybe it's Spooner's washtub," someone said.

"Maybe," said someone else, "but Spooner isn't in it."

And I said, "Let's haul it up and have a look at it."

So that's what we did. We hauled it up. It was wet inside, and it was empty—except for one thing resting in the bottom: There, in a shiny puddle, lay an object made from what looked like the ribs of some kind of flatfish, or so it seemed to me. Its downward teeth were pure and white as ivory, and across its back it was studded with little colored stones and bits of gold. I lifted it out and held it up, and we gazed at it, wordless. Then Leech came up and took it out of my hand. "It's a comb," he growled. "A mermaid's comb. Put it back in the washtub, mates, and set the tub adrift. For it doesn't belong to us. The doughhead will be wanting it back, him and his mermaid."

We did as we were told, and then, it was the

strangest thing. Leech leaned at the rail for a long time, watching the washtub float off, and he had a look on his face like dreaming. We moved away and left him to it, and on the days that followed, we didn't speak of Spooner. Not in front of Leech, at any rate. For we didn't know how to ask him the question we wanted to ask, and didn't dare to, anyway, for fear he'd throw us overboard. But I can tell *you* what that question was, since Leech is nowhere near, and here it is. How did he know a mermaid's comb when he saw one?

———

AFTER A few moments of silence while everyone thought it over, Mrs. DelFresno said, "Do you believe in mermaids, Mr. Plank?"

"Well," said Jack, "I don't *not* believe. Here's the way I see it. If a man like Leech thinks they're real, then who am I to doubt?"

"He sounds like a rude, ill-tempered man," said old Miss Withers. "But I suppose there might be a soft spot in him somewhere."

"I've come to think there is," said Jack. "Soft as molasses cake."

"Molasses cake is a splendid thing," said the uncle of old Miss Withers. "Are you sure you don't want to be a baker?"

"Yes, I'm sure," said Jack. "I was good at soup, you know, but that's not the same thing at all."

"Never mind," said Nina. "We'll think of something else."

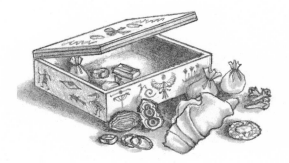

4

NOT
A FORTUNE-TELLER

ON THE third night, at supper, Nina reported that she and Jack Plank had been down to the docks. "We saw a Gypsy woman telling fortunes for the sailors," she said, "and afterwards, they gave her a little bag of money."

"That's the way it works," said the uncle of old Miss Withers with a giggle and a snort. "She tells a fortune, and gets a fortune back!"

"Uncle," said old Miss Withers severely, "don't try to be amusing. As you very well know, these Gypsies have a dangerous skill called 'the power of the eye,' and they're not afraid to use it. They can cast spells, and raise ghosts, and do all sorts of witch-ridden things. The only way to deal with them is to keep them away. Far away from respectable people."

"Perhaps," said Mrs. DelFresno, "but I've always thought the fortune-telling part sounded good."

"That's the part Miss Nina thought I should try," said Jack. "We talked it over. But finally we had to let it go. In the first place, I don't look right. Wasn't born to it. And then there's the fact that I don't have any idea what's going to happen *tomorrow*, let alone ten years from tomorrow. The rest of it—casting spells and raising ghosts—well, if I'd known how to do all that, I might have been more help to poor Victor Mack."

"This Victor Mack," said the uncle of old Miss Withers. "Was he troubled by ghoulies?"

"We didn't know *what* troubled him," said Jack. "At least, not in the beginning."

———

BEFORE HE turned to pirating, Victor Mack had been across the ocean on a trader that was working the far coast of Africa. Later, when he'd left all that behind and joined us on the *Avarice*, a few of us were with him on his first night, down in the hold—Leech and Stovehouse and four or five others—and he showed us a little wooden box he'd picked up over there, all carved with strange-looking symbols. And he let us see the treasures he kept in it: spices from India, and gold Arabian earrings, and he had a piece of agate from Syria and two rubies all the way from Burma. But he also had a thing that was wound around with linen. He said it was the hand of an ancient Egyptian mummy that he got from a peddler on some island dock. "I laid down plenty of gold for this," he told us proudly. "It's rare, so keep your hands off. The peddler said the wrappings should stay wrapped. And he told me to hide it so it wouldn't get snatched."

Somebody said, "Snatched? Who'd want to snatch a mummy's hand?"

"Maybe the mummy's ghost," said someone else.

"I know whose hand it is," said Victor. "The peddler told me." He took the thing out of the box and held it up. It looked as if there might well be a hand inside, but what with the windings of the cloth, it was hard to picture. Someone asked if it was green and withered, but Victor said he'd never unwrapped it to see.

"So whose hand is it, then?" Leech asked him.

"A king from back in olden times," said Victor. "When they used to turn kings into mummies. I can't say the name out loud because then he might hear me, and he'd know where it is."

"Who might hear you?" Leech asked him. "Some king? Dead a thousand years and he'll *hear* you? You can't believe that rubbish. Throw the whole thing overboard, is my advice."

Stovehouse said that holding on to dead things was a bad idea, anyway—that dead things ought to be buried. But Leech growled out, "Except when you want to cook them for supper. Eh, Stovehouse?"

We laughed at that, but Victor wasn't laughing. "This hand is worth a lot of gold, I tell you," he said in a low and angry voice. "Throw it overboard?

Never a chance of that. And if you don't believe the king was real, I'll tell you his name. Amemsees, that's what. His name is Amemsees. He's famous over there. His hand was chopped off by one of his wives—I don't know what *her* name was—because she was mad at him about something. She hurled it out the window and somebody grabbed it and ran away. Maybe some ancestor of the peddler. Everyone knows the story."

"Well, well," said Leech. And then he grinned and roared out, "HEY THERE, AMEMSEES! HEY, KING! WANT YOUR HAND BACK?"

"Hush up that racket!" hissed Victor with a terrible frown.

But Stovehouse said, "Cool off. There won't be any ghost. Why, here I am with only one leg, but I never had an itch to go looking for the other one. And I never will, alive or dead. If your mummy's ghost has any sense left, he'll feel the same."

"Well, maybe," said Victor, but he was still angry. He tucked the hand back into his little box, which finished off the subject.

I thought it was the finish, anyway. But after he'd

been with us for a week or two, Victor began to change. There was something about his manner that seemed to say he was worried, and more than just a little. One night at supper he said we ought to get a cat. A black cat. Well, of course, a lot of people think black cats bring good luck to ships, but we'd never had one. Leech always said they made him sneeze. Victor looked uneasy when he heard about that, but there wasn't any way to change it. Then, the next day, he complained that Stovehouse wasn't smashing the eggshells flat before he threw them overboard. "It's dangerous," he said in a jittery voice. "We'll get in a shipwreck for sure." And he took to wearing one of his gold Arabian earrings. He said it would save him from drowning.

Now, either you hold with things like this or you don't, is mostly the way it goes. Leech, for instance, always said anyone who believed such stuff was dead from the neck up. But there were a few of us—well, we weren't so sure. And so, when Victor wasn't any- where around, we discussed it. We wondered if a mummy's hand was risky. At last, one night, we went to Victor and tried to get him to talk. "What do you really know about that thing?" we asked him. "What if it *is* haunted? Maybe you should unwrap it. See if it looks dangerous. Then you could throw it overboard, like Leech suggested." But Victor said he had the box hidden and wasn't going to unwrap the hand for anyone. And he certainly wasn't going to throw it overboard—not when he'd laid out all that gold to buy it. And then he said there wasn't any trouble, and he'd thank us to leave him alone.

Well, we left him alone, but the trouble didn't. Over the next day or two, it got a lot worse. He'd let out a gasp if we came on him unexpected, or go pale for no reason we could see, and put his hands over his ears as if to keep from hearing things. And then, one morning, the mate who'd been on watch the night before reported that he'd seen Victor sneaking around in the dark on deck, his eyes as big as binnacles, as if he was looking for something he was scared to death he'd find.

When it was night again, moonless and breezy, I

was the one on watch. And Victor finally opened up to me. He crept out of the shadows, and he edged close and whispered, "Jack, did you hear it? You *must* have heard it! It was banging around down there, and then it went away. I think it came up here. Help me, Jack! Which way did it go?"

"I'd help if I could," I whispered back, "but I didn't hear a thing. What did you hear?"

"It seemed like a sort of a voice," said Victor, peering over his shoulder into the dark. "It made a wheezing sound. Well. I don't know. I'm not sure." He pulled back then, as if he didn't want to talk about it after all. "Never mind," he said. "Never mind." And he edged away along the deck and disappeared.

And then in fact I did hear something: a kind of heavy breathing that seemed to fade — slowly — after a minute or two. But there wasn't anything there. Nothing you could see, anyway. "It's probably only the water," I told myself. "Waves, and an extra bit of wind." But I confess I found myself wondering if maybe we *should* get a cat.

Then, on deck in the morning, Leech growled to

a few of us, "Look up there! Just look where that poor chump Mack has stashed himself. He's turned stark-staring loony, is what. He'll fall and we'll have to scrape him off the deck with an oar."

We looked, and indeed there was Victor, high above us, propped against the masthead. He'd climbed the ratlines, and he looked as if he meant to stay where he was. Leech went for Captain Scudder, who tilted his head and glared upward. "Mack!" he hollered. "Get out of the way of that rigging and come down right now. Come down, or we'll have to shoot you down." But Victor might as well have gone deaf. He didn't move a muscle. The captain sighed and turned to me. "Plank," he said, "go up and try to talk to him. We don't want to shoot him unless we have to."

So up I went, and when I got to where Victor was holding on, I told him, "You'd better come down."

He was gray-faced, but he looked determined. "I can't," he told me. "There's something after me. I'm sure of it now. When I came away from you last night, I went back down to the hold and tried to go to sleep, but it seemed like my hammock was getting pushed, and there was that same wheezing sound in my ear. Up here, though, I'm safe."

"Not if they have to shoot you, you're not," I told him.

But he only shook his head and held on tighter.

I thought for a moment, and then I said, "Look here, mate, I wasn't going to tell you this, but now I guess I'd better. Last night, on watch, I did hear something. There wasn't anything to see, but I did hear something. It sounded like breathing. It sounded like a ghost."

Color rushed back to the poor man's face. "Jack!" he cried, grabbing my arm, which made him teeter on his footing. "Jack, I knew it was real!"

"It's real if ghosts are real," I said. "If they are, you must be right about that king. Maybe he does want his hand back."

Victor set his mouth in a hard line. "Listen," he said. "I bought that hand fair and square. It's mine now, not his."

"I don't think ghosts care about fair and square,"

I told him. "But come down. I'll stay with you, and we'll figure what to do."

So he came down, slowly, hand over hand along with me, and when we got to the bottom, I said to everyone, "Victor's been having nightmares, but he'll be all right. I'll take him below and sit with him till he sleeps."

It was dim in the hold, and no one was around. We dropped down on a bench among the hammocks and were silent at first. Then, finally, I said, "I've heard about ghosts. They only cause trouble when they want something. In spite of what Stovehouse said, there's one around here, all right, and it's got to be the ghost of that king of yours. Amemsees. He probably heard Leech shouting to him. Maybe that's how he found us. But that doesn't matter. What matters is, he must want his hand back. What else could he want? But he doesn't know where you've hidden it. Victor, you have to give it back."

"Blast it!" said Victor. "Double blast it! This whole thing is that big-mouth quartermaster's fault. Still, it's only a ghost come after me, Jack. If I don't let on where I've stashed the hand, what can happen?"

"What can happen?" I said. "That ghost can go on haunting you forever, that's what can happen."

When he heard this, it was clear he was wavering. What to do! But at last he squatted down on the floor and pulled up a loose board. "It's under here," he told me. And he lifted the little box from beneath the board and held it out. And that was the moment when we heard the sound. All at once it was coming towards us—the wheezing, the heavy breathing—rushing at us out of nowhere.

"Open the box!" I cried. "Right now. *Hurry!*"

The sound swept down on us, louder now, engulfing us. With trembling hands, Victor opened the little box. And when he did, he was flung over backwards, and the box dropped to the floor.

There was a sharp, surprising moment of total silence. And then there came a sound like—what was it like? The closest I can come is to say it was the sound of disappointment. Bitter disappointment. "AAHHHhhhh!" Then it trailed off and was gone, and the whole thing was over.

Victor sat up and rubbed the back of his head. His

box lay open and his treasures were strewn about, but as for the hand, some of the linen wrappings he had guarded so closely lay unwound and loose, there on the floor, and poking out from what was left was nothing but a twig from a tree branch—a broken bit with parts sticking out like fingers. It didn't even seem to be an *old* twig.

We goggled at it, both of us too out of breath to speak, but at last Victor reached out and picked the thing up. "I can't believe it!" he rasped. He was all anger now. "This isn't a mummy's hand. It isn't *any* kind of a hand. That peddler took my five gold florins—*five* of them, I tell you—and this is what he gave me! A blasted piece of a tree!"

"Now, wait a minute," I said. "It was a bad deal, yes, but on the other hand, the part about Amemsees was true. That was a real ghost, Victor. And *he* thought the hand was in there, too! Didn't you hear how disappointed he was? Don't forget that. That's something, anyway. Poor ghost."

Victor stared at me with his mouth open. "Poor ghost? *Poor ghost?*" he exclaimed. But then, all at once, his anger petered out and was gone. "Don't tell the others what happened, Jack," he said. "Promise you won't tell them."

"If you don't want me to, I won't," I said. "I'll just say you decided the hand was too much trouble and so you threw it overboard. Go and do it now. Throw it overboard. And that way I'll only be telling the truth."

So that is what he did.

———

EVERYBODY AT the supper table thought about this for a minute or two, and then Nina said, "It's strange, though, how the ghost was fooled. I thought ghosts knew everything."

"Maybe not everything," said Mrs. DelFresno, "but you'd certainly expect it to know its own hand."

"Why should anyone expect a thing like that?" said old Miss Withers scornfully. "A ghost is only what's left of a person when the outsides are gone. And if the person it used to be was a bonehead, well, then, the ghost will be a bonehead, too. What else?"

"My dear," said her uncle, "that's a very interesting notion. What you're saying, then, is that the king—that king, Amemsees—must have been a bonehead."

"Of course he was," said old Miss Withers.

"I like it!" said her uncle. "A boneheaded king!"

And they talked about it all through supper.

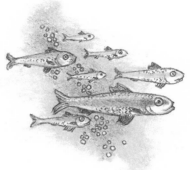

5

NOT
A FISHERMAN

"MR. PLANK, perhaps you should be a fisherman," said Mrs. DelFresno on the fourth night as everyone gathered in the dining room. "You must know all about boats and bait."

"We talked about that today, Miss Nina and I," said Jack. "But I don't like taking things out of the water."

"Come, come, Mr. Plank," said old Miss Withers. "There's no other way to get fish that I ever heard of."

"In fact," said her uncle, "we're having fish for supper. Octopus."

Jack looked alarmed. "Maybe you misunderstood," he said. "An octopus isn't a fish."

"Well, whatever it's called," said the uncle, "I know one when I see one. I watched this afternoon while Mrs. DelFresno cut it up and took off the . . ."

"No, no, don't speak of it!" cried Jack. "You don't understand!" And then he frowned and shook his head. "Forgive me," he said. "I'm being foolish. You haven't heard about Figley, so how *could* you understand?"

———

IT WAS Stovehouse who told us the story, one night aboard the *Avarice*. It had happened on a different ship in a different place, he said, at a time when he still had both his legs and didn't have to cook. They had taken on men from a plundered ketch, and one was a fellow who kept his distance from everyone. His name was Simon Figley, an odd duck, tall, bony, and suspicious, strung up so tight he'd have cracked if you looked at him sideways. Figley was sent below to the galley, which suited him very well, for he flat out refused to be up on deck. He said he'd work for the cook down there, but he wouldn't do more. He said he hated ships, but couldn't go anywhere else. He wouldn't say why. That kind of talk didn't make him friends, of course, and everyone ragged him, early on, but he paid them no mind, so that after a while they left him to himself.

And then one night, for some reason, Figley got sick to his stomach. Stovehouse was on watch at the time—it was two o'clock in the morning—when here came Figley pounding up from belowdecks, bare as the back of your hand, to hang his head over the rail.

The night had started cloudy, but while Figley leaned there, the sky came suddenly clear and the moon, round and newly full, rode free. This was when it happened. Figley straightened up in that magical light and shook himself, and let out a kind of moan. And then, while Stovehouse stared, he began to change. His shoulders sank and his two arms went to four long tentacles curling right down to the deck, while his legs made four more of the same. And his body and his head swelled up and came together into a bag-like mass. It was a smooth change, said Stovehouse, syrup-smooth, and frightful. Worse than frightful. For Figley had turned into an octopus. And not just some piddling runt of an octopus, either, but a big one with tentacles five feet long.

The creature glared at Stovehouse with owlish eyes, and then, turning away on its eight reaching arms, it slid to a gunport at the rail, slipped through, and dropped into the sea.

Stovehouse, of course, was struck all of a heap. He'd never seen anything like *this* before, and didn't know what to do. Still, his turn at watch had some hours yet to run, so he waited by the rail, thinking that Figley or the octopus, one or the other, might well come back. Nothing happened for a long time, till at last the moon went down, and its glow went down behind it. And then, sure enough, there came a rush of bubbles, and *whoosh!* Figley, back to his

normal self, burst sputtering to the surface of the water. He seemed pretty much worn out, and hardly able to swim. So Stovehouse threw over a line and hauled him up.

Neither of them spoke a word. Not then, and not the next day, either, or any day thereafter, though Stovehouse told us he could feel Figley's eyes on him sometimes, and confessed that he often returned the glance when Figley wasn't looking.

He didn't tell his shipmates anything. He didn't like to, somehow, he said, for it seemed it was nobody's business but Figley's. But—business? What kind of business was a thing like this? He told us he'd heard of men changed to wolves sometimes by the light of a full moon. We'd heard of that, ourselves. And yet—an octopus? If he hadn't seen it happen with his own two eyes, said Stovehouse, he'd have called it the nightmare of a ninny. The fact was, however, he *had* seen it happen, and so he decided that when the moon was back to full, he'd take night watch once more and see what he could see.

At last the time came round. The ship, of course, had not just lain at anchor in the month gone by but had kept its course along the seacoasts just as it always did, looking for plunder. Still, it was everywhere winter in that part of the world, a time when the full moon rose only a little later than it had the month before. So Stovehouse was hopeful. Surely he could watch the change again — Figley's frightful change! But when he went out on deck into a breezeless night, there was the moon already, a great bright circle high in a cloud-free sky, with Figley nowhere to be seen. Either the whole thing *was* a nightmare, and he was the ninny who'd dreamed it, or Figley had made the change early and was gone.

Stovehouse was cursing his luck when all at once, near the ship, he noticed a commotion in the sea that was beading the surface with bubbles. He leaned far over the rail to see if it was Figley. Leaned a little farther. And leaned out farther still. And lost his grip and fell. Yes. Stovehouse fell into the sea, plunging deep, headfirst and horrified.

Down he went, and then, with an effort, looped around and tried for the surface. The water above him was dim-lit with moonlight, the ship's hull a dark shape of safety not far away, and he aimed for it, kicked for it, eagerly. But—what was this, this other shape moving in between, this dark and dangerous shape with its lashing tail? This great fish raiding a school of herring, flinging them to its mouth with that tail, churning the water into all those glittering bubbles Stovehouse had noticed from the deck? He said he could tell we'd guessed, and guessed it right: a shark.

So now what could he do? His kicking had caught the shark's attention. It paused and looked at him, and grinned, with shreds of herring hanging in its teeth. And then it started towards him. Stovehouse said his prayers, preparing for the worst.

But the world is full of surprises. The shark had started towards him, and then it simply stopped. For arms had grabbed it, arms were flung around it, arms on its tail and fin. Sure and powerful arms, and eight of them. The octopus.

At once there was a battle. The herring fled, and Stovehouse, with no breath left, went straight for the surface of the water while, beneath him, the sea was whipped to foam. He splashed his way to the ship's stern, where he clung to the rudder, gasping, till at last he could holler for help. But the battle was over almost before it began, so that by the time his mates were there to haul him up, the foam had disappeared and the sea was back to calm. The battle was over, and no way to tell who'd won it. The whole thing, start to finish, from the moment he fell to the moment he was back on deck, had happened, said Stovehouse, in perhaps five minutes, while the moon sailed on, serenely unconcerned.

Shark or octopus, one, of course, had triumphed. Figley himself was gone, that much was clear, and he never returned. So perhaps the shark had swallowed him whole. Or swallowed the octopus he was. But no, said Stovehouse, somehow he was sure that Figley had carried the day, as the saying goes, and then was gone to the bottom of the sea, to the octopus world of caves and lobsters, where the moon could make no difference.

———

"AND OF course he may still be down there," said Jack. "So you see why I can't eat an octopus. What if it's really Figley?"

Nina nodded, and then she said, "It's good what he did about the shark. Maybe he was thanking Mr. Stovehouse for keeping his secret."

"Maybe, but it all depends," said Jack. "Did the octopus think with Figley's thoughts? Or only the thoughts of an octopus? *I* don't know. Do you?"

No one seemed to know for sure. And then the uncle of old Miss Withers, leaning towards Jack across the table, said with interest, "But of course your cook got his leg chewed off by the shark."

"Who? Stovehouse?" said Jack. "Not at all. Stovehouse lost that leg long after, plundering. The shark had nothing to do with it."

"Oh," said the uncle, leaning back again.

"As for octopus," said Mrs. DelFresno, "I'm afraid I did fix one for supper. But we'll all understand if you avoid it, Mr. Plank. You can make a meal from the vegetables."

So that was the end of that.

6
NOT
A BARBER

ON THE fifth night, at supper, the uncle of old Miss Withers rubbed a hand across the top of his head where there wasn't any hair worth mentioning. "I'm thinking of getting a wig," he announced to everyone. "Something long and curly. And I might even grow a beard."

"There was a rich man on the street today in fancy clothes," said Nina, "and he had a long, curly wig. He didn't have a beard, though."

"You don't see many beards these days," said Jack. "Nobody seems to like them anymore."

"And a good thing, too," said old Miss Withers. "I've never understood why a man should want to look like a goat. So—probably the barbers are busy. You should learn to be a barber, Mr. Plank. Very respectable work."

"We talked about that today, Miss Nina and I," said Jack, "when we saw the man with the wig. But—I don't know. It sounds very demanding. Snip, chop, scrape, all day long, trying hard to please the customer, with here and there the doctoring a barber has to do. I don't think it's my kind of work at all. And on top of everything else, I'd always be thinking of Boris and the crab."

———

BORIS BILSKI had a beard when he came to us on the *Avarice*—a nice long black one. He was a Russian, and he'd always lived in the north of his country by the Baltic Sea—if you know where that is. His job was to sweep the streets of Saint Petersburg up there and he had his own broom for the work. His beard and his broom—that's all he did have.

And then, a little while ago, the king—well, they don't call it "king" in Russia, but I can't remember what they do call it—anyway, the king over there decided beards are old-fashioned, and he said everyone would have to shave them off or else pay a fine to keep them. Boris couldn't bear to part with his beard, but he didn't have money for a fine. So he left Saint Petersburg and joined the crew of a British ketch headed home from her northern trading. He figured no one aboard would object to his beard, and he was right about that. But on the other hand, they wouldn't let him keep his broom. Some sailors think old brooms bring bad luck to ships. So the broom had to go, but at least he kept his beard. And after this and that experience, here and there, he ended up on a brig we plundered near Martinique, and we took him on for crew.

Everyone liked him. He was a simple fellow, content with his life—though he wished he had his broom back. And now he was a pirate! He could scarcely believe he would get a share of the plunder. "Am I to be rich?" he asked us. And we told him maybe, if he managed to save his shares, which was more than most of us could do. But he said he would try very hard, so that someday he could buy a new broom.

Things wagged along till the time came round, as it always does sooner or later, to scrape the hull of the *Avarice* clean of seaweed and barnacles. We happened to be near a safe little inlet called Coxon's Hole, at the far end of Cuba — and there we dragged the *Avarice* ashore, heaved her over, and settled down to work.

And then, at the end of that first afternoon, with the tide heading out, Boris and I and two or three others splashed into the shallows for crabs, so Stovehouse could cook them for supper. But Boris was new to crabbing. He leaned too far down to find them, with his face almost into the water, and a very small crab, alarmed and hurrying to save itself, climbed into his beard by mistake. Boris straightened up and cried out something Russian, like "Shto etta," I think it was, and tried to pull the creature loose. But the more he tried, the more it tried not to let him, and it climbed in deeper, and it got more tangled, till there was nothing he could do but stand there with a beardful and listen to his shipmates laughing.

The solution seemed clear enough—just cut off the beard, and the little crab with it. But Boris shook his head. What? First, no broom, and now, on top of that, no beard? So I went and fetched the sailmaker, a patient fellow called Needles, and he and Boris sat down face to face, each on a basket, and Needles began to draw those chin hairs aside, one by one, to clear the way for the crab without any damage to the beard. It was delicate work, and even after an hour or so, the crab was still partway covered and still clinging tight, half trapped, half afraid to let go.

At last the quartermaster, Leech, came down to look at the situation. "This whole thing is foolishness," he growled after watching for a bit. "Cut off that beard, mate, *now*, and be done with it."

But Boris pulled back, his hands flung up to his chin. "No, no!" he cried. "Never!"

Leech looked disgusted. "Don't go all of a twitter,"

he said. "Beards do grow back, in case you didn't know. If you don't cut this one off, that crab will die and start to smell something awful, right under your very nose. And its corpse will be hanging there till doomsday."

This was not a happy thing to think of. Still, it was clear why Boris felt the way he did. We all need something to call our own, after all. And how could a new beard ever take the place of his old one, worked on so hard for so long, and now so dear and familiar? Boris got to his feet, hunched and sad, and wandered along the shore, talking to himself, with the crab swaying under his chin.

What happened next was sudden, noisy, and disorderly. Out from the underbrush burst a squealing guinea pig and, hot behind it, a hungry wild boar. The guinea pig, with its sharp little claws, ran right up over Boris's pants leg and onto his shirt, and the boar, hardly pausing, knocked the poor man down. Well! We shouted and rushed to save him, beating at the boar with whatever we could find, and stabbing at it, too, with knives and daggers, for a boar's

got tusks that can tear you to ribbons. There was too much confusion to do it much harm, but six of us were more than it could handle, so at last it grumbled off, back into the underbrush. But the guinea pig? The guinea pig had fastened itself to Boris. It had grabbed his beard, right on top of the crab, and it wouldn't let go.

We helped him to his feet, and we all stood there gasping and catching our breath and, on top of that, trying not to laugh when we looked at him. But you can imagine what a sight he made. And at last Leech said, with uncommon gentleness, "Bilski, you see how things are. There's no other way. Sharpen your knife and shave yourself, the sooner the better." And then he went back to the work on the ship.

Boris just stood there, swamped, while the rest of us picked up the baskets and turned again to gathering crabs. But when I glanced at him over my shoulder, he was sitting on a rock, scraping at his chin with his dagger. And when I glanced again, crab and guinea pig—and beard—were gone.

Well, poor Boris! And yet, his story had a happy ending. Two happy endings, if it comes to that. It happened that Needles had kept a wig he'd grabbed once at a plundering. And he turned that wig into a kind of beard, long and curly, with hooks of a sort to go over the ears and hold it on, and when it was finished, he gave it to Boris. "Here's a trifle to cover your chin, mate, while the new beard's growing in," he said, and Boris was delighted. He wore the thing for months, and looked very elegant, too — so elegant, in fact, that two or three others in the crew wanted trifles like that of their own, though I don't think Needles ever made another.

And as for the other happy ending, it turned out that the guinea pig wasn't gone at all. Boris had put it inside his shirt, and afterwards he kept it for a pet. He took great care of it, too. So, though at first he had only beard and broom, at the end he had beard, broom, and guinea pig. Yes, in time he bought another broom, and a fine one, too. Of course he did. As often as not, the wind blows just the way it should.

———

"I DO like happy endings," said the uncle of old Miss Withers.

"Except," she said severely, "you must know, Uncle, those villainous wigmakers chase little children about the streets and cut their hair off—quite literally steal their hair—to make their product."

"That was true for a long, long time," said Jack. "You're right, ma'am. But now it appears they much prefer horsehair, which is good because I don't think a horse would mind losing a little of its mane or tail."

"Not being a horse, however, you can't be sure of that," said old Miss Withers.

"No," said Jack, "but I do think a horse could drive away a wigmaker any time it wanted to."

"Of course it could," said Mrs. DelFresno. "But let's leave it at that, now, and settle to our supper, shall we?"

So they did.

7

NOT
A GOLDSMITH

ON THE sixth night, the uncle of old Miss Withers brought a guest to supper. "Here's Chummer, bless him!" he said, introducing the guest. "Known him for years." And they all shook hands.

"My uncle has mentioned your name a time or two," said old Miss Withers, looking at him disapprovingly. "It appears you were a man of substance once. What happened?"

Mr. Chummer didn't seem to mind the question. He was very tall and very thin, and had rather a squint to his eyes, and he leaned down to old Miss Withers politely. "Today, ma'am, I'm in the coffee trade," he said. "I used to be a goldsmith, but the tide turned against me."

"Still, a goldsmith is a true artist, Mr. Chummer," said Mrs. DelFresno. "What very nice work it must have been!"

"Oh, yes!" said Nina. "That's what you should do, Mr. Plank!"

"Thank you, my dear," said Jack, "but I'm no artist. And anyway, there seems to be very little gold these days for making much of anything."

"That was the trouble exactly," said Mr. Chummer with a sigh. "Not enough gold. One way or another, it all went off to Spain. Still, I can't say I miss the work. The customers I had were a jittery lot. Gold can do strange things to people."

"Strange indeed," said Jack. "Once, down in southern waters, we came across a man who said he was a sailor from a merchant ship, but his story was very dark, and in the end . . . well, perhaps you'll tell me what you think."

———

WE WERE cruising along at twilight, just off the coast not far from Cartagena, when the watch called out that there was someone on the nearest beach — a solitary man waving his arms and shouting in an effort to be heard above the racket of the surf. So we went as close as we could get, dropped anchor, and sent a boat to bring the fellow in.

When we got him aboard, he looked weak as a rag. "Thank you, thank you," he gasped. "I'm very much obliged. I was sure I'd be dead before another hour went by." He was small and shabby, with a tooth broken off at an angle in the front of his mouth, and he seemed the kind of man who would go a long way to stay out of trouble. Nevertheless, his eyes were sharp. As he spoke, his gaze slid over us, one by one, as if to see what we were made of.

One of the men who'd brought him on board took Captain Scudder aside and muttered something in a low voice. "Oho!" said the captain. He turned to the fellow, who was sprawled on the deck, leaning against a bitt. "I think," said the captain, "you'd better show us what you've got there, mate, hidden in your shirt."

The fellow looked surprised for a fraction of a moment, and then gave the captain a smile around the broken tooth. "I was just about to do exactly that!" he said in a whiny sort of voice. And he pulled from his shirt a pendant suspended from a length of common string tied around his neck. It looked like a frog standing up on hind legs and wasn't more than two inches tall. But it was solid gold. It gleamed in the last of the light, and it was very beautiful.

Captain Scudder leaned down and took the little thing to study it, and then he handed it back. "I've seen pendants like that before," he said. "They're very old, and they're worth a lot of money. We'll give you something to drink, and then you'd better tell us where it came from."

It was a story I'll never forget as long as I live. The fellow's name was Snipe, he told us—English-born, but recently a sailor on a Spanish ship called the *Rosa* that had broken from a merchant fleet one night in a heavy fog, a month or so back, and slipped away alone to look for gold. "The crew was wild for it," said Snipe. "You've seen that kind of attitude, of course. They couldn't fix their minds on anything else. The plan was to search all through the caves hereabouts where the natives hid their treasure long ago, trying to save it from—well, from people like us. But the caves have been searched since then, you know, time and time again. Myself, I didn't see how there'd be anything left to find. Still, I had to go along with it. What else could I do? We went ashore in groups here and there, up and down the coast, to get one more good look before the *Rosa* came back to pick us up. There were three in my group, me and Carlos and Brazzo, put down on that very beach where you found me tonight."

Snipe paused then, and rubbed his face wearily. "We brought along plenty of food," he said at last, "but my mates didn't care about that. Their hunger was in their heads. We found a string of caves straight off, all empty except for piles of bones, most likely the bones of those natives who'd had their treasure grabbed. But then, later on, we came to another cave, off by itself around the side of a hill, where there weren't any bones. By the light of torches, we pawed through heaps of dirt and stones, and found at last a rotting wooden box. Well! It showed me up for a fool, because there was a fortune in that box: hundreds of coins, gold and silver both, and more than that, little figures like this one I showed you, with the heads of animals. Frogs. Turtles. Fish. Some with the horns of deer, some that looked like crocodiles. I never saw anything like it."

Snipe took a swallow from the mug of beer that Stovehouse had given him. As for the rest of us, we waited, watching him. He took a second swallow, and then put down the mug and shook his head. "Brazzo reached into the box," he told us, "and lifted up handfuls of coins. And he said the whole thing ought to be ours because we'd done the work to find it. He said we shouldn't have to share it with the rest of the crew. And Carlos agreed. That was against our system, though, which was always share and share alike. I didn't like it, but I didn't have a choice; I had to go along. What else could I do, a little man like me?"

"You did a lot of going along, it sounds like," said Leech, with his growling laugh.

Snipe shrugged and repeated, "I didn't have a choice." For a moment, he looked away and sucked on his broken tooth. And then he went on: "The two of them made a terrible plan. They decided that when the *Rosa* came to pick us up, one of us would be waiting on the beach to shout that the fever had struck us, old yellow jack itself, that one was already dead, and that if the crew on shipboard wanted to stay free of it, they'd better get away as fast as they could and leave us to our dying. Brazzo said they'd run for sure, and when they were gone, we could divvy up the gold and hide it in our clothes and boots. And then, when some unknown ship came by, we'd signal it to pick us up, explain that we'd been stranded, and ask to be taken to the nearest port. And once we got there, we could go our separate ways, each with a ruddy fortune."

There was silence for a moment or two, and then Leech said impatiently, "Well, so what came of it? Where's your share of the gold?"

"Here's what happened," said Snipe. "The *Rosa* came to get us late one afternoon, and Brazzo sent me down to scare it off. Everything went just right. One mention of yellow fever and the *Rosa* burned the breeze and was out of sight in no time. Then Brazzo said we could split up the gold in the morning, so we ate our supper and washed it down with rum, and afterwards, in the cave, with the box of treasure waiting, we stretched ourselves out and went to sleep. But when morning came, Carlos was lying there dead with his own knife in his chest, and half of the gold was gone."

There was a lot of mumbling from the *Avarice* crew at this. Leech said, "It was a beetle-headed notion, keeping that gold from the rest of your shipmates. Something bad was bound to come of it."

But Snipe only shook his head and said, again, "What could I have done against the two of them? Of course, Brazzo thought I'd murdered Carlos, and I thought Brazzo had done it. He said to me, 'Where'd you hide the gold?' And I said, 'No, where did *you* hide it?' At last we more or less agreed it had to be natives who came to do the deed and take away the gold—natives waiting somewhere in the jungle. Brazzo said they'd come back for sure, so we'd better split what was left in the box and get ourselves to safety. We buried Carlos and we stayed on the beach. But all day long the sea was empty. No other ships appeared."

"So the natives came back after dark?" asked Captain Scudder.

"They must have," said Snipe, "but *I* didn't see them. When it was night, Brazzo said we'd have to stay awake, both of us, and watch each other while we watched for natives. And that's what we tried to do. But at last, towards morning, it started to rain. It was peaceful, and I guess by then I thought we were safe, because I fell asleep. But the natives were there, all right, and when I woke, Brazzo was dead, like Carlos, with his dagger in his chest."

"Very quiet natives," said Leech.

"Well, yes," said Snipe, "they were."

"And the gold?" asked the captain.

"Gone," said Snipe. "Every scrap. Except for this

one little pendant that was lying half buried in the dirt at the mouth of the cave." He pulled it out of his shirt again and stared at it. And then he said, "So that's my story, mates. The pendant is yours if you want it. With my thanks for saving my life."

"No," said Captain Scudder. "Keep your gold."

"Well, then," said Snipe, "I know you don't go into ports. Too dangerous. But if you're willing to take me as near to one as you can, I'll swim or wade ashore. I want to go home to England, and I'll sell the pendant to pay my way."

By this time, it was late in the night and safely dark, so we took him north along the coast towards Cartagena and lowered him overboard at an inlet. We never saw him again. But we couldn't stop talking him over, him and his doubtful story. Not an hour would go by but what someone would raise a question: Why didn't the natives kill Snipe when they killed the other two? If there weren't any natives, and Snipe did the killings himself, where did he hide the gold? If he did hide the gold, would he leave it for a while, or would he go back at once to fetch it? And if he did go back, how would he get there?

At last Leech got impatient for answers. He shaved off his mustache, dressed up in clothes from a plundering, and rowed himself to the docks at Cartagena. And when he came back, this is what he told us: Number one, a man had come into a trader's and sold a gold frog pendant. And number two, a man had bought a little yawl, and told the dealer he was sailing south along the coast to find a friend.

"And so," said Leech, "what now? He's gone for the gold, of course, the miserable faker, and he'll get it, too, if we don't lay hold of him."

"Unless he's off to England, the way he said he'd be," said Captain Scudder. "Anyone can buy a yawl. That didn't have to be Snipe."

We argued and debated, and finally the captain said, "All right. We'll go and look. It's the only way to put an end to this." So we eased back down along the coast to Snipe's beach, and a group of us went ashore. But Snipe wasn't there, and neither was the gold. There was nothing to find but the body of a man with a knife in his chest. Brazzo. We buried him, and we left that place behind, steering away west, out to the open sea.

Leech wasn't satisfied. "We could have found him, him and all that treasure," he insisted. "If you'd only had a little starch in your gut, you pikers, we'd have spotted that ketch and grabbed the gold without a blink. Why, that's what we do best of all! We're really good at that! And now it's too late." And he mumbled to himself for days.

But after a time, he came to accept it. "All right, mates," he told us, "you had it your way." And he added, in a whiny voice like Snipe's, "I didn't have a choice! I had to go along. What else could I do?" And then, with one of his growling laughs, he went below and had a glass of rum in the galley, and said no more about it.

———

"WELL," SAID Mr. Chummer after a moment's thought, "it seems to me that this fellow Snipe was most likely innocent of everything."

"Indeed he was not," said old Miss Withers firmly. "I knew from the very first he would turn out a cheat and a rascal."

"What do you think, Mr. Plank?" Nina asked him.

"At the time, I watched him, and I listened to every word," said Jack, "and was never sure one way or the other. I'm still not sure."

"And I, for my part, can't be sure you'll like the supper I've made," said Mrs. DelFresno. "So let's begin and see how it all measures up."

They did, and agreed that the supper was perfect, but they never did agree about Snipe.

8
NOT
AN ACTOR

ON THE seventh night, the uncle of old Miss Withers said, "That troupe of players is in town again."

"Yes, we saw them today, Mr. Plank and I," said Nina, "parading with their posters. It must be fun to be an actor, and get all dressed up in a costume to make people happy."

"Happy!" said old Miss Withers. "Just as often, they want to make you *un*happy." And then she looked severely at Jack. "I hope you're not considering such so-called work as that, Mr. Plank," she said.

"Well, to tell you the truth, ma'am, we did talk it over," said Jack. "I agree with Miss Nina. It all looks very pleasant. But it's not a thing just anyone can do. You have to know how to make people believe you're somebody else."

"A fellow I used to see sometimes didn't have a notion who he was," said the uncle. "So he had to make himself up. And he told me he liked himself perfectly well that way."

"I knew a little girl once who was sort of like that," said Jack. "But when things were straightened out, she settled down quite nicely. Except there was a moment when she had to do some good acting. Or so I understand."

"I'm glad you understand," said old Miss Withers. "I don't."

"Well then," said Jack, "here's the way it was."

WE DROPPED anchor once, at an island way east of here, to get fresh water. We'd been plundering, and hooked a lot of treasure, but we'd drained our barrels dry. Plundering is thirsty work, and you can't drink gold. So a few of us towed the barrels in to shore, and there we found seagulls—I never saw so many in one place—nesting and fishing and wheeling about, hundreds of them, and when they saw us, they raised up a whacking great fuss. But water belongs to everyone, and when you need it, you don't take your hat off and beg a bunch of birds to let you by.

So we pushed on through and searched out an inland stream with a helpful fall of good fresh water, where we started to fill the barrels. And then, all at once, here came a wild-haired little girl all draped in rags and feathers, making a terrible face at us. We figured if a child was there, not more than five or six years old, there must be other people somewhere near. So we asked her, one of us said, "Hello, little girl! Where's your family?" But instead of answering with words, she backed up, flapping her arms hard, and shrieked, *"AW! AW! AW!"* I swear, you'd have thought *she* was a seagull. And when she made that noise, three of the real birds came out of nowhere, shrieking themselves, and swooped at us, trying to drive us off. Then the little girl laughed and skipped away towards the beach, merry as you please, and the gulls calmed down and followed her.

Now, here was a puzzle and a half. We talked it over and decided to finish with the barrels and then have a parley with our shipmates to figure what to do about the child. For we didn't see another human soul, and didn't like to leave her there alone.

So back we went, rolling the barrels to where we'd left the dory, and saw the little girl in the midst of an uproar of gulls, all of them screeching *AW AW AW*, fighting over a big dead fish of some kind, trying to push each other off so as to grab the best bites. The little girl was holding her own, too. She pushed and screeched with the best of them, and wasn't at all put down.

When we told our mates about her, back aboard the *Avarice*, they all had questions, of course. How had she come to be there? Why wasn't anyone with her? How would we get her away? If we did get her away, what would we do with her? And Leech, well,

Leech growled that the whole thing from start to finish was the biggest load of wish-wash he'd ever heard in his life. If she was happy on the island, let her stay there. It was none of *our* affair.

For a few minutes after that, no one dared to offer much in favor of the child, but at last Chesstree—young Billy Chesstree—kind of cleared his throat and said if we wanted, he could ask his grandma to help. "My grandma's genteel as you please," he told us, "but she ain't stiff. I think she'd see to the little tyke and raise her proper if we paid for the extra expenses."

"If she's so genteel," said Leech, "how come she puts up with *you*?"

"I'm the only grandson she's got," said Chesstree with a blush. "She thinks I'm matchless."

There weren't any other suggestions, so at last, with the captain's permission and Leech with his lip still curled, a few of us went back to the island and fetched the little girl, her shrieking *AW AW AW* the whole time, while the gulls wheeled and dove around us, and when Leech saw her, he said she was nothing but a useless bit of flotsam washed up from the sea. We called her Flotsam after that, and we gave her the best bites at every meal. Well—but we had to do that. We weren't just being generous. If we didn't, she'd scream that terrible scream and grab what she wanted, while Leech sat back looking disgusted.

But it was nice to have her there, you know. I taught her a word or two, and we sang her songs at bedtime, and pretty soon she was content enough. But the thing that seemed to calm her most was that three of the seagulls stayed with us. They were perched in the rigging and wouldn't be shooed away, and they kept an eye on her—and us—every minute.

Chesstree's grandma lived a good way back to the west, at a place called Saint Ann's Bay. So the next time we were anywhere near, we anchored at night just off the coast, and Chesstree and a few others rowed little Flotsam in to shore and delivered her to Chesstree's grandma. And they told us afterwards that it looked ideal from the start. Grandma Chesstree took to Flotsam right away, and promised to give her a bang-up raising. "She won't be called Flotsam, though," said Chesstree. "Grandma told us that wouldn't do at all. So her name will be Flora." And then he added, "Remember those seagulls? Well, they followed us all the way in, and when we left they were settled on my grandma's roof."

I never saw Flotsam—or Flora—again. But her story went right on unfolding, and here's what happened. Whenever we were anywhere near Saint Ann's, Chesstree would slip ashore and visit at his grandma's, and slip back after to report, early on, that Flotsam was happy, later that she was learning words, then that she could sing like a lark, and then that she was turning out well-favored, with shiny hair and bright brown eyes.

Then, with a good long time gone by, Chesstree came back to the ship after one of his visits and reported that in only two weeks Flotsam was going to be married. She was fourteen, after all, and a rich man on the island had arranged with Grandma Chesstree for Flotsam to marry his son. And he told us his grandma was expecting him to be there for the wedding. "She'd like you all to be there," he told us, "but she knows that might be dangerous."

We sent Chesstree back that very night, because

his grandma was right: It was safer if we went on our way before someone noticed we were out there. "But take the girl a present from that chest in the hold," said the captain. "A necklace or a silver pot. And something for your grandma, too. And we'll pick you up next time we're back this way."

A half a year went by before we came to Saint Ann's again. A couple of mates rowed in by moonlight and were soon back on board with Chesstree himself between them, all three grinning ear to ear. "What's this?" we said, gathering round. "What's all the joking about?"

"No joking," said Chesstree. "I haven't come back to stay. The thing is, mates, I've up and married Flotsam."

After we'd whooped and slapped him on the back, someone asked, "But what about the son of the rich man? What happened to all of that?"

Chesstree told us everything. His grandma had invited the boy and his ma and pa to supper the night before the wedding—a rare and fancy supper with two kinds of fish and three kinds of fruit, and rice and potatoes and a lot of little cakes. But when it was all on the table, with everyone behaving well-brought-up, Flotsam all at once sprang to her feet and flapped her arms and made those screeches she always used to make, and she pushed the guests aside and grabbed the best bites for herself. And not just for herself, because she took as much as she could carry outside to the seagulls—those same three seagulls—they've never left her for a minute—and they screeched and fought and ate together, the four of them, happy as you please. And the boy and his ma and pa were so horrified, they canceled the wedding on the spot and stomped off home, sore as crabs.

Leech maintained it wasn't a bit surprising, considering how Flotsam was raised. "That girl will always be half seagull," he said.

"Maybe," said Chesstree. "But afterwards, she claimed she did it on purpose. She'd have done it, she told me, whether I was there or not, for she didn't want to marry that boy. She said she'd be Mrs. Billy Chesstree, or never get married at all."

We laughed at that, and poked him in the ribs, and

Leech said, "Just the same, you've gone and married a seagull, mate. Feathers in your breakfast—that's the way of it. And those three birds will round out the family. They'll be with you a long, long time, you know, to see you behave yourself."

But Chesstree stood his ground. "That's all right with me," he said. "I'm not opposed. Because, the thing is, we're happy as can be." And then he blushed and added, "I know I'm nothing special, but Flotsam likes me. In fact," he said, "she thinks I'm matchless."

———

"I WONDER where Flotsam came from," said Nina after a moment or two. "Did you ever find out?"

"No, we didn't," said Jack. "She didn't know, herself."

"Poor thing!" said Mrs. DelFresno.

"Maybe not," said the uncle of old Miss Withers. "That friend of mine, the one that made himself up, he thought it was a first-rate situation. No relatives to tell him what to do."

"Why, Uncle!" said old Miss Withers with a frown. "What kind of talk is this?"

"Oh, well," said her uncle quickly, "if he'd had *you*, my dear, he'd have known what a fine thing relatives can be."

To get past this in a hurry, they all turned at once to eating their supper, till at last Nina said, "I wonder if Flotsam's seagulls are still keeping watch."

"I'm sure they are," said Jack.

Nina nodded, and then she put it aside. "Well, on with the list, Mr. Plank," she said. "We'll hit on something."

"Maybe," said Jack.

And Nina said, "I'm sure of it."

9

NOT
A MUSICIAN

ON THE eighth night, old Miss Withers brought in a friend named Mrs. Lamb. Mrs. Lamb was shy; she held a handkerchief up to her face and blushed behind it while old Miss Withers introduced her to everyone.

"I've brought Mrs. Lamb to supper in order to raise her spirits," said old Miss Withers in a take-charge voice. "There was another of those accidents upriver today, and she's letting it get to her."

Everyone wanted to hear what had happened,

but Mrs. Lamb was in no condition to describe it herself, for as soon as old Miss Withers said the word "accidents," she drooped and, with both hands, pressed the handkerchief over her eyes as if to hold back tears. "Straighten up, Maria," said old Miss Withers firmly. "Death comes to us all."

"Who died?" asked her uncle with interest. "Someone we know?"

"Not exactly," said old Miss Withers. "It was a goat—a goat who lived next door to Mrs. Lamb. It escaped from its yard somehow and wandered off to the marshes where the crocodiles are. You know the place. And when it came near the water, one of those ugly brutes grabbed it by the leg, and no more goat."

Mrs. Lamb made a little sobbing sound into her handkerchief. However, the uncle of old Miss Withers didn't seem to care about goats. "Nothing unusual in a thing like that," he said with a yawn.

"But crocodiles don't set out to be brutes," Nina protested. "It's just they have to eat, like everybody else. Maybe there are some mean ones here and there, but they're not all bad. I was recommending to Mr. Plank today that he might want to be a musician, and he said no because of a shipmate who played the flute, and had friends who were crocodiles!"

"Well, at least," said Jack, "he was friends with one particular crocodile."

Mrs. Lamb took the handkerchief down from her face. "I play the flute," she whispered.

"That's so," said old Miss Withers. "She does."

"Ah, well, in that case," said Jack, "my shipmate, Waddy Spontoon, would have valued your company, ma'am."

———

WADDY HAD been aboard the *Avarice* from the very beginning, longer than any of the rest of us. He was getting pretty old. But he knew every inch of the ship from stem to stern, and there was plenty he could do that was needed. He gave a hand to Stovehouse in the galley, chopping vegetables and plucking chickens, things like that. And he knew how to sharpen a sword and load a cannon. But Waddy was important to the crew in a much more particular way: He knew how to make music. Sometimes after supper, when the moon was high and everyone was drowsy, he would get out that flute of his and play the tunes that give a person peaceful dreams when it's time to go to sleep.

One day when we'd been cruising through the Caymans — those islands west of here, you know — the wind went calm and there was nothing to do but find a place to hide and wait it out. We towed the ship to a little cove, and a few of us tramped inland up a stream to see what we could find for supper. Waddy was with us, and we hadn't gone far before he tripped on something and gave a bad twist to his ankle. We told him to sit and ease it and we'd come back for him later. So that's what Waddy did. He plunked himself down and leaned against a tree, propping his ankle on a hump of roots, and then he took his flute out of a pocket and began to play. After a few minutes, though, he had this funny feeling that someone was looking at him, so he peered around, and up and down, and then at the stream sliding by beside him. And that's when he saw the eyes and the nose of a crocodile, sticking up above the surface of the water, hovering there, watching him.

Well! Waddy dropped his flute and tried to roll away from the water's edge. He'd have gotten to his feet to run—he *tried* to get to his feet and run, he told us—but his ankle didn't want him to, so he just half-lay, half-sat there, wondering what the crocodile would do.

He didn't have long to wait for an answer. The crocodile climbed out of the water and stood there with that look they have on their faces sometimes, which is almost a smile. It stood there next to Waddy's flute, and it smiled. And then it smiled some more. And then, at last, it gave a little bit of a bellow.

When a crocodile bellows, even when it bellows just a little, the sound is enough to rouse up the Devil. Well, you've heard it, of course. It's like barrels with rocks in them rolling down a tunnel, is what I think. Waddy said he pretty much decided he was doomed, except then he noticed that the crocodile had lost a few teeth. In fact, he noticed that the crocodile was definitely not young. And the more he studied it, the more it seemed a little simple-witted in a kindly sort of way. And all at once he felt a kinship with the creature. "It was old, like me," he told us. "We had a lot in common." So he reached out and took back his flute, and then he sat up and began to play a tune.

This was exactly the thing to do. Once in a while, somehow or other, we hit on exactly the thing. For, in fact, the music was just what the crocodile wanted. It sighed a loud sigh, and then it sat down, there beside the stream—well, lay down, I suppose—and smiled, with the end of its tail waving ever so slightly, and listened to Waddy on the flute. Waddy played all the tunes he'd ever learned, and still the crocodile listened and seemed most remarkably contented. So Waddy was starting over with his list of tunes when the rest of us came back along the stream bank, and when we saw the crocodile there with Waddy, we naturally assumed there was danger and yelled to

him that we'd save him. But Waddy waved his arms and yelled back, telling us to swing by off to one side, that the crocodile was friendly, and not to do it any harm. We did what he said, of course. Still, all the yelling and general racket was enough to alarm the beast, for it slipped back into the water and disappeared. And we figured that would be all.

Later, though, after supper, when the day's work was done and we'd bandaged Waddy's ankle good and tight, we were lounging on the deck of the *Avarice* when we heard it. From up beyond the inlet, among the darkening trees, the crocodile was bellowing once more. The sound echoed down along the stream and out to the moonlit ship with a note of longing in it, somehow. "Listen to that!" said Waddy. "It's my croc. Poor solitary fellow, he wants me back."

In the morning, the ship was still becalmed and must stay where it was, hidden at the edge of the trees. No plundering for us without a friendly wind. So Waddy said to Captain Scudder that he'd like to go back upstream and spend an hour or two with the crocodile. "He's all by himself, alone, you see," said Waddy. "And the time, well, it tends to drag. That's the way things are when we get to be old, as you'll see for yourself someday. I could take him some fish for breakfast, and we could have a last bit of music."

There was a sadness in Waddy's voice as he said all this. Captain Scudder noticed it, of course, and patted him on the back, and said he should go ahead. So we put him ashore, with a stick to use for a cane, and off he went inland, limping slowly along the banks of the stream, with a couple of fish hanging from his belt and his flute tucked into a pocket.

The day was half gone before Waddy came back, and he didn't seem sad at all anymore. He was just—as you might say—filled up with thought. He would nod, and then he'd shake his head, and then he'd say "Humph!" and "Fancy that!" as if he'd seen something out of the common run. And at last we said to him, "Waddy, for goodness' sake, aren't you going to tell us what happened?"

This seemed to wake him up. "Oh! Well!" he said, and then went on: "I've had a morning and then some, mates. A morning and then some. I'll tell you if you really want to hear." So we gathered around to listen.

He had gone to the place where he'd seen the crocodile, and he'd played a tune or two as a kind of signal. Nothing happened. So he kept on going upstream, stopping now and then to send out more signals. No response. But then, after three or four miles, the water widened out into a swampy kind of pond. "If you'd gone that far, mates, yesterday," he told us, "you'd have seen what I saw. And heard what I heard, too."

For the swamp was home to a family of crocodiles: a few big ones and some that were small, sunning themselves or just being friendly and sociable. Until they caught sight of Waddy. When that happened, there was a moment of surprise, and then two of the big ones, ever so silently, slid into the water and headed straight for him. He didn't know what to do, he told us, so he pulled out the flute and played a hasty little phrase of music.

Once again, it was exactly the thing to do. For no

sooner had he played that phrase than from the other side of the pond came a bellow to split your ears. One bellow, two, and then a third. The crocodiles in the water stopped where they were, and every head turned to see what must have been the fearful lord and master of them all.

"And it was my croc, mates," Waddy told us, his face all pink with delight. "I knew him right away, and he knew me. That good old fellow! Lonely? Not him! Not simple-witted, either. He heard my music, and he came straight out from the reeds and mosses, followed by a wife or two, and they all made way for him! They moved back and they gave him room! And he swam across the pond to me, and he climbed out, and he smiled. When he smiled, another of his teeth fell out, but so what? Nobody cared in the least. I served him the fish I'd brought for his breakfast, which seemed to please him, and then I sat down and I played my flute. I played for a long time. And he closed his eyes, and smiled, and listened. It was a fine morning, mates. I'll never forget it." And with that, he moved off along the deck of the ship, mur-muring to himself, nodding, and full of wonder.

The wind came back later in the day, fresh and strong, and we sailed away to our plundering. But Waddy had a talk with Captain Scudder, and told us after supper that he meant to leave the business of pirating and go back home up the coast to the colonies, to the place where he was born. He wanted to make his living by playing his flute, if that was possible, and, he added, he might even take himself a wife. "If my crocodile can have a wife," he told us, "why—then—so can I, mates. So can I. It's never too late to be happy."

———

"WHAT A good man your Mr. Spontoon must have been," said Mrs. DelFresno. "Do you know if he really went home to the colonies?"

"I hope so," said Jack. "And I like to think he's joined a little group and is playing his flute all the time. It sounds like a fine life, doesn't it?"

"If it's as fine as all that," said old Miss Withers, "why aren't you a musician?"

"I would be if I could be, ma'am," said Jack. "But I have no ear at all for music. I can't sing my way through tra la la." And then he added humbly, "A person has to have the gift. Like your friend here, Mrs. Lamb."

And Mrs. Lamb was so pleased to hear she had the gift that she put her handkerchief up to her face again. But not to cry. This time she was hiding a smile.

10

HOW THE PROBLEM
WAS SOLVED

EARLY ON the morning of the ninth day, Jack Plank climbed out of bed and went to the window to see how things were. Blue sky, blue water, docks already busy—everything was just the same as ever. But Jack was not the same. His heart was heavy as he leaned there, looking out. "My time is up," he said to himself. "I tried the best I could, but there's no work here in Saltwash for the likes of me. I don't know how to do a blessed thing, and that's the truth. I'll have to go back to sea. Maybe, if I was a common sailor, some ship would take me on. But oh, how I hate to leave this friendly house! Dear me. Dear me." He turned away from the window, and with sighs and shakings of his head, he washed himself, and brushed his hair, and packed his little trunk. And then he clumped down the stairs to the kitchen, where he hoped to find Mrs. DelFresno.

There she was, indeed, mixing up batter for pancakes, and she nodded to Jack when she saw him in the doorway. "Good morning, Mr. Plank," she said. "You're just in time for breakfast. The bacon is ready, and pancakes are on the way." And then she noticed how sad he looked. She put down her mixing spoon and said, in a softer voice, "What's this, now? Is that your trunk I see there? Surely you can't think of leaving us!"

"I'm afraid I must, ma'am," said Jack. "My time has come to an end, and my money is nearly gone. I tried to find work, with Miss Nina helping most patiently and kindly, but there was always something wrong, you know. Some reason why one thing or the next wouldn't fit. You saw as much yourself as the days went by. So it's back to the sea for me, where I belong."

"Oh well, belonging!" said Mrs. DelFresno. "That can mean a lot of different things." She smiled and picked up her spoon again. "We'll have our breakfast, and then we'll see," she told him. "Go and take your place, please, while I pour out the pancakes."

In the dining room, old Miss Withers and her uncle were already sitting at the table, each at work on half a grapefruit, while Nina laid out plates and forks for the pancakes. "Hello there, Plank," said the uncle. "There's plenty of grapefruit. Want some while we're waiting?"

"Oh—well—no, I guess not," said Jack. "I'm not very hungry this morning."

"You should eat while you can," said old Miss Withers firmly. "One never knows when bad luck might take over."

Jack felt that this was true, but all he could do was nod. "Yes, ma'am," he said. And then he pulled out his chair and sat down. "The thing is," he told them, "I've really only stopped to say goodbye. I'm leaving this morning. Going back to sea. But before I go, I want to tell you how fine it's been to have your company—you, and Miss Nina, too."

Without looking at him, old Miss Withers waved her grapefruit spoon and said, "You're not going anywhere."

"It's kind of you, but all the same, the time has come," said Jack. "I'm sorry for it, more than I can say, but that's the way things have to be."

"No, they don't," said old Miss Withers.

At this exact moment came a knocking at the door. Nina hurried out to the hall to answer it, and in a moment she was back, bringing with her Mr. Chummer and Mrs. Lamb. "Good morning, all," said Mr. Chummer, and Mrs. Lamb managed a shy smile.

"It's sort of a party, Mr. Plank," said Nina to Jack. "For Mother's pancakes."

"Yes, indeed," said Mr. Chummer. "For the pancakes, you know. Can't let a thing like that go by!"

And so Jack ate his breakfast after all. He felt that it was strange somehow, a party for pancakes. And it did seem as if they were looking at him rather more than necessary. But—well, they were only being pleasant, he decided. Extra pleasant because he was leaving so soon.

When everyone had had enough, and the pancake platter was empty, Jack pushed back his chair and started to stand up. But Mrs. DelFresno, seated next to him, put out a hand to his arm and said, "Please, Mr. Plank, do stay where you are. The thing is, this isn't really a party for pancakes. It's for you, and it's not to say goodbye. We want you to hear a suggestion. It was Nina's idea, but all of us think it's the very thing. And we're all here to beg you to consider it."

"The very thing?" said Jack. "The very thing for what? I don't understand."

"We have a job for you," said old Miss Withers. "Work. Something for you to do."

"But that's exactly the problem," said Jack. "Goodness knows I've tried, but there's nothing I *can* do."

"Nonsense, man," boomed Mr. Chummer. "You do one thing very well indeed, and it's a thing that everybody likes."

"Don't you see, Mr. Plank?" cried Nina, clapping

her hands. "Why, you're a storyteller! That's what you are! You've given us a fine time, with all the tales you've told."

"You even cheered up Mrs. Lamb, you know," said old Miss Withers, "with that drivel about the flute and the crocodile."

Mrs. Lamb nodded her head. "But it wasn't drivel," she whispered.

"And so," said Mrs. DelFresno, "here's what we want to suggest. Three afternoons a week, right here, we'll have a story time. You'll tell a tale, and everyone will come to listen. We'll charge a small fee, for you and me to share, and afterwards serve tea. And while the guests are eating, Mrs. Lamb will play the flute."

Mrs. Lamb nodded her head again and smiled an enormous smile.

"We have a sign," said Mrs. DelFresno. "Nina made a sign. Bring it in, dear, and show it to Mr. Plank."

Nina went out to the hall and came back with a sturdy, flat panel of wood on which she had painted, neatly:

JACK PLANK TELLS TALES
TUESDAYS, THURSDAYS, AND SATURDAYS
AFTERNOONS AT FOUR FOLLOWED BY TEA
MUSIC BY MRS. LAMB ON THE FLUTE
3 SHILLINGS

And at the bottom, she had painted a picture of a seagull.

Jack sat back in his chair, astonished. He could scarcely believe what he had heard. He gazed around at them all, and at last he said, "But—my stories—they're only little things, you know, that happened once upon a time. I'm glad you liked to hear them, but surely, other people—well, what I mean is—"

Old Miss Withers interrupted him. "See here, Mr. Plank," she said. "It's no use your making a fuss, for it's all decided. Stories aren't much, of course, but on the other hand, they're not so little, either. And if we liked them, so will other people."

"Yes, other people will," said Mr. Chummer. "We're very sure of that. Saltwash needs a man like you, Mr. Plank, to brighten up its days. We want it to be your home. How does the saying go with you sailors? We want you to make the harbor."

"Run into port," said the uncle of old Miss Withers.

"Find moorings," said Nina. "Please, please, say yes!"

"We think," said Mrs. DelFresno, "that this is where you belong."

———

AND SO the problem was solved and settled. Jack never ran out of stories; in fact, the more he told, as the weeks went by, the more he seemed to remember. And the people in Saltwash never got tired of hearing them. Then, too, as he settled in at Mrs. DelFresno's boardinghouse, he made himself useful in many little ways, chopping wood and carrying heavy things about. Sometimes he even made soup. And somebody said, a year or two later, that he'd married Mrs. DelFresno and become a second father to Nina. Well, that may be so, and maybe not. There's been no reliable report. But it seems to be sure that, as Waddy Spontoon pointed out, it's never too late to be happy.